My Real Rabbit

GERALDINE WITCHER

Illustrated by Branwen Thomas

SCRIPTURE UNION

By the same author
Stowaway Adventure – *6–8s*
Runaway in the Den – *Tiger* series
The Den Gang Goes Green – *Tiger* series

© Geraldine Witcher 1996

First published 1996

Scripture Union, 207–209 Queensway, Bletchley, Milton
Keynes, MK2 2EB, England.

ISBN 1 85999 028 2

British Library Cataloguing-in-Publication Data.
A catalogue record for this book is available from the British
Library.

Phototypeset by Intype London Ltd
Printed and bound in Great Britain by Cox & Wyman
Ltd, Reading.

Contents

With special thanks to the Rogers family for giving me the idea and letting me use their names.

Lively Arrives

Mike woke up. Stevie was screaming again. Every night Stevie screamed.

"Shut up, Stevie," Mike groaned.

The door opened and Mum came in. She talked to Stevie and cuddled him. Soon he was asleep again. Mike reached out for Peter Rabbit.

Peter Rabbit was a little stuffed toy rabbit, with a blue jacket. He was just like the one in the story. He had always been Mike's favourite toy. He had taken him everywhere. He had even taken him to school in his bag until he got used to it. Mike drank camomile tea, because that's what Peter Rabbit in the story did.

But Mike was seven now. He had stopped playing with Peter Rabbit, though he still liked camomile tea! Now he only had him at bedtime. Mike had always had Peter Rabbit in bed with him ever since he had been given him. He had been given Peter Rabbit the day Stevie was born. He always cuddled Peter when he woke up in the night or when Stevie disturbed him in the night. Peter helped him go back to sleep.

So now, he turned over, pulled the duvet up round his ears and hugged Peter tight. Soon he was asleep too.

The next morning, Stevie was very tired. So, after breakfast Mum put him, and baby Rachel, back to bed. That left just Mike and Mum. Mike enjoyed himself. He and Mum made flapjacks. Then they went into the garden, to hang the washing out. Mike could just reach to put the pegs on.

"You are getting tall. You're my big, helpful boy," Mum said.

Mike smiled. He felt important. Stevie wasn't big enough to help with the washing.

"Mike," Mum went on, "do you know why Stevie screams at night?"

"I think he has bad dreams. I used to sometimes," Mike said.

"But you didn't scream."

"I had Peter Rabbit," Mike said.

"I wonder if that's what it is? Stevie didn't scream when he had his 'blanket' to suck. Maybe he still needs something to take to bed," Mum said.

When Stevie had been very small Mum had put a little piece of cloth over his pillow in his cot. The cloth stopped the pillow getting dirty. Stevie had got into the habit of sucking a corner of it. They all called it his "sucky blanket". When he started walking it had been funny because he trailed it around with him. Sometimes, it got tangled up in his feet and he fell over. When baby Rachel had been born, Stevie had given her his "blanket". He said he was too big for it now he wasn't a baby any more.

That night, Stevie screamed again. Mike remembered what Mum had said. He slipped out of bed.

"Look, Stevie. Here's Peter Rabbit. If you cuddle him, you won't have bad dreams," he said.

He pushed Peter Rabbit into Stevie's arms. Stevie stopped screaming. He smiled. Then he closed his eyes.

Mike went back to bed. It took him a

long time to get to sleep without Peter
Rabbit. Once he had gone to sleep he didn't
wake again till the morning. Stevie was still
asleep. He had one arm round Peter Rabbit.
It works, Mike thought.

He did not want to wake Stevie, so he
got out of bed quietly and tiptoed out of
the bedroom.

Downstairs, Mum was feeding baby
Rachel.

"Where is Stevie?" she asked.

"He's asleep," Mike replied.

"He didn't scream last night," Mum said.

"He did. But I gave him Peter Rabbit and he stopped," Mike said.

"You gave him Peter Rabbit? But he's your bedtime toy," Mum said.

"I don't need him as much as Stevie does," Mike said. "He stopped him screaming."

"That's wonderful! It was lovely to sleep all night without being woken up. Thank you, Mike," Mum said.

Mike smiled. He felt good.

That night, Stevie didn't want to go to bed. Mike was downstairs, watching television. He could hear Stevie crying and Dad's voice getting cross. Mike got up and went to the door.

"Dad!" he called up the stairs. "Stevie can have Peter Rabbit."

"Are you sure?" Dad called back.

"Yes!" Mike yelled. He just wanted Stevie

to be quiet, so that he could watch his TV programme.

Suddenly, it was quiet. Dad came in and gave Mike a hug.

"That was a very kind thing to do, Mike. Stevie is happy now," he said.

Mike smiled. It was nice being grown-up.

"I don't need him any more. Stevie can keep him," he said.

"Keep who?" asked Mum, coming into the room.

"Peter Rabbit," said Mike. "He stops Stevie crying. And I'm too old for him now."

"I hope he stops him screaming again tonight," Mum said.

And he did. From that night Stevie didn't scream.

At the weekend, Mum said, "I think a boy who is too old for Peter Rabbit, might be old enough for a real rabbit. Don't you think so, Mike?"

Mike stared.

"You mean me? A real rabbit for me?" he asked.

Mum nodded.

"Yes, I think you're big enough to look after one. Shall we go and get one after lunch? We can leave Stevie and Rachel here with Dad."

"Yes, please!" Mike couldn't believe it. A real rabbit of his very own!

He rushed out into the garden to tell Dad and Stevie.

After lunch, Mum and Mike went to the pet shop. It was fun going shopping just with Mum. The pet shop was exciting. There were gerbils and hamsters in cages. The baby hamsters were asleep all together in a big heap.

"They look like an old fur hat!" Mum said.

There were lots of bright coloured fish swimming around in big tanks. But Mum went past them to the back of the shop.

They went down some stairs into another room. There were big cages in here. Mike wrinkled up his nose. It did smell funny. It's like when we went to the zoo, he thought.

One cage had kittens in. They were asleep in a heap, just like the hamsters. Another cage had two little black puppies. One of them was jumping up at the bars of the cage and barking – little yappy barks. The biggest cage of all had baby rabbits in it!

Mike rushed over to the rabbits' cage. Which one should he choose? There was a lovely black one. There was a white one with black spots. There was one with very long, floppy ears. And there were two little brown rabbits.

He stood watching them for a long time. The black one kept scrabbling at the side of the cage with its front paws. The little brown ones were playing. They chased each other around the cage, then rolled over and over together. Then one jumped up and ran away and it all started over again.

"I want one of those little brown ones," Mike said.

Mum went to get the shopkeeper. He told Mike that the brown ones were Dwarf rabbits.

"They will never get very big. Dwarf rabbits don't grow very much," he said.

Mike thought a rabbit that stayed small would be nice. At the moment it was even smaller than Peter Rabbit.

"How big will it get?" he asked.

"About this big," the man said, holding his hands apart.

That's just about the same size as Peter

Rabbit, Mike thought. Then my toy rabbit and my real rabbit could be friends. So he said, "I would like one of them, Mum, please."

They bought a little brown baby rabbit. Mum bought some rabbit food too.

The shopkeeper put the rabbit in a big box with holes in the lid. Mike held it very carefully all the way home. He could feel his rabbit moving inside the box. Sometimes he saw its little black nose pushed up against one of the air holes. Sometimes it scrabbled at the cardboard.

When they got home, Mike put the box on the floor and opened the lid. Dad and Stevie came to see. The rabbit hopped out and sat on the floor. It twitched its nose.

"What is it doing?" Stevie asked.

"It's smelling. Rabbits twitch their noses nearly all the time," Mike said. He was pleased that he remembered what the shopkeeper had told him.

Suddenly the rabbit hopped across the room. Its little white tail bobbed up and down as it went. It ran under the table, jumping over the chair legs to get there. Then it hopped round by the fridge. Stevie jumped out of the way. Mike ran to catch it but every time he put his hands down, the rabbit hopped over them and escaped.

"My goodness, it's lively!" said Dad.

"That's a good name. I think that's what I'll call it – Lively, my very own rabbit!" Mike said.

Lively's Home

Lively enjoyed exploring the kitchen. She ran under the table and sat there with her nose twitching. She enjoyed jumping over things. She went over the chair legs and back again lots of times. She took a really big jump over Stevie's legs. Then she hopped across the floor to the cooker. She stretched up on her back feet and sniffed at the door. Then she hopped all the way round the edge of the kitchen, sniffing at the cupboards as she went. At last she curled up on the doormat and went to sleep.

Mike thought she was wonderful.

"My real rabbit! My very own real

rabbit," he whispered.

He was so glad he had given Peter Rabbit to Stevie.

"Now we must make her a real home," said Dad.

"Come on, Mike. Put her back in the box for now. She can have a rest. She looks tired. Close the box properly so she can't escape. Now let's go into the garage and make her a hutch," he added.

"Stevie come too?" Stevie asked hopefully.

Dad looked at Mike. Mike was feeling good and grown-up, so he said, "Yes, but you must only watch. It's my rabbit, so I've got to make the hutch."

Stevie nodded and they all went out into

the garage.

In the garage there were all sorts of exciting things. Of course the car lived there, and all the bikes. The front of the garage smelt of petrol from the car. The back of the garage, where Dad had his workshop, smelt of wood and paint. Here, there were bits of wood, pots of paint, rolls of wire and all Dad's woodworking tools too. Mike and Stevie were not usually allowed to touch these things. When Dad was working there, sometimes Mike came out to pick up the wood shavings. The wood fell in golden curls and smelt lovely. Mike bent down to pick up a bit now. It was twisted up tight like a spring. Mike uncurled it. It was smooth and so thin it was almost see-through.

"I think Lively would like a bed made of wood shavings," Mike said. What fun it would be to lie in a golden heap of sweet-smelling curls.

"I think you're right. It would be a good way to use them up too. Perhaps Stevie could collect some up for us?" Dad asked.

Stevie smiled and crawled under Dad's workbench, where the best shavings were. He started making a big pile.

"Now we need some good strong bits of wood for the hutch. The floor must be nice and thick. Come on, Mike. See what you can find," Dad said.

Mike and Dad sorted through the wood. It was fun. The wood smelt nice. Some of it had wavy lines on. The wavy line bits were smooth but other bits were all scratchy. Dad explained that the wavy line bits were cut with the grain of the wood. The other scratchy bits were cut across the grain.

"It's all to do with the way a tree grows. Remember how they have rings all round the trunk? Well, the grain lines are the rings. If you cut across the tree, so you can see a whole ring, you get rough bits. But if you cut up the tree, you can see the marks of each ring as it goes up the tree. That's how you can get the wood really smooth," Dad explained.

That was hard to understand. But Mike remembered the tree stumps they had seen where trees had been cut down in the wood. They had counted the rings to find out how old they were. He thought trees were very clever. They had round rings in their trunks, but when they were cut, the rings made a pattern of wavy lines and squiggles.

At last, Mike found a bit just the right size for the floor. It had a nice pattern on it too. Dad picked out some more pieces to make the back and one side of the hutch.

"Now we need some thin bits to make the other sides. Then we can fix wire netting to them so that Lively can see out," said Dad.

Mike could not find any pieces like that. He was just going to give up. Then Stevie pulled out a long thin bit from underneath Dad's workbench.

"This one?" he asked.

"That's just right, Stevie. We can cut it into pieces. They will make the other sides," said Dad.

"Well done, Stevie," Mike added.

They got to work. Dad sawed and glued and nailed. Mike and Stevie held the bits together till the glue was dry. When all the wood was fixed together, Dad went to the back of the garage. Up on the wall was a roll of wire. He got it down and began to unroll it.

"Be careful, boys, this is very scratchy. Chicken wire is horrible stuff," he said.

"Why is it chicken wire?" Mike asked.

"I don't know. I suppose it's because it's what people use to make chicken runs," Dad said.

"Then this bit is rabbit wire," said Mike.

Dad unrolled it, then he cut it with a big pair of wire cutters. It made a sharp pinging noise. Then he fixed it on to the hutch with little hook-shaped nails. They trapped a bit of the wire and held it down on to the wood. Then Dad bent all the loose ends in towards the wood.

"That way they won't hurt you or Lively," he said.

Soon they had a lovely hutch. It had a covered bit for Lively to sleep in. Mike let Stevie put all the wood shavings he had gathered in there. It would make a lovely soft bed. There was a place for Lively to play too and for her to have her food.

They took the hutch into the house. Mum gave Mike two bowls. One was for Lively's food. The other one was for water. Then he went to get Lively. When he picked her out of the box she wriggled. It was hard to hold her. He was glad to put her down in her hutch.

"You must pick her up a lot. That way, she will get used to it. Then she won't struggle," said Dad.

"And you must remember to keep her water bowl full," said Mum.

'Tomorrow I will make a run for her in the garden. You will have to remember to move it around. If you don't she will eat all the grass in one place. Then we won't have a lawn any more," Dad said.

"Why can't she just run in the garden like we do?" Mike asked.

"She might get lost. She might get into a fight with a cat. She might eat the flowers. All sorts of things. She's safer in a run."

"There's so much to remember. I didn't know looking after a real rabbit was so hard," Mike said.

Dad smiled.

"We bought Lively for you, so now she is your responsibility," he said.

"That's a long word. Besponsablity. What does it mean?" Mike asked.

"When God made the world, he told the

first man and the first woman that they must look after the world. They had to look after the plants. They had to care for the animals. They had to love and help their children. It was their responsibility. We still have to do that today. For every child we have, we have to look after it the way that is best for it. And it's the same for animals that we look after,' Dad explained.

"Like you and Mum look after baby Rachel and Stevie and me?" Mike asked. "Rachel needs more sleep than I do, so Mum makes sure she gets it. I sometimes need help with my school work, and you and Mum help me with that."

"That's right. God made families so that children could be loved and cared for. He asked people to care for the animals, too," Dad said.

Mike looked at Lively. She was eating her food. She looked happy. Her nose was still twitching.

"I will try to look after her properly. She's my rabbit. She's my responsibility," he said.

Lively and Peter Rabbit

Mike turned over in bed. It was still dark. What had woken him up? Oh no, he thought, Stevie is crying.

Mike climbed out of bed. He went over to Stevie's bed. As he came near, his foot hit something soft and fluffy. The soft fluffy thing rolled away.

"Oh," said Mike. "You've dropped Peter Rabbit. I've just kicked him under the bed."

"No, the big dog has eaten him!" wailed Stevie.

"No, he hasn't. You've been dreaming."

But Mike shivered as he said it. He didn't like the big dog. It lived over the road

behind a big wooden fence. Every time
Mike or Stevie went past, the dog barked
and growled at them. The noise came
through the fence far above Mike's head.
He had never seen the dog, but he knew it
must be enormous!

Mike bent down and picked up Peter
Rabbit.

"The dog hasn't eaten him. He's here," he
said. He gave him back to Stevie. Stevie
cuddled one arm round Peter Rabbit. He
put his other thumb in his mouth. He went
back to sleep.

Mike went back to bed. He curled himself up under his duvet and tried to go to sleep. But he couldn't! When he shut his eyes, he saw the big dog barking and snarling.

Without thinking, he reached out for Peter Rabbit. But Peter Rabbit wasn't there. He was in Stevie's bed.

"I need Peter Rabbit. I can't sleep without him. He's mine," Mike muttered to himself.

He slipped out of bed again. He went to take Peter Rabbit from Stevie. But Stevie was still cuddling him tightly.

Mike stood in the middle of the bedroom floor. There were other toys lying around him. He could just make out their shapes in the dark. There was Rachel's big pink elephant. There was his own floppy clown that Granny had made him when Stevie was born. But he didn't want them. He wanted Peter Rabbit!

Peter isn't mine any more, he thought sadly. I gave him away.

But Lively is, he remembered. I'll get Lively.

So he tiptoed to the door. He could see light coming through where it wasn't quite shut. Mum had left the hall light on. Going downstairs wasn't too bad. But crossing the dark kitchen was horrible.

Lively's hutch was by the back door. There was some light coming in through the window. Mike could see to open the hutch. He picked up the sleepy rabbit.

She snuggled into his arms as he raced back to his bedroom. Back in bed, Mike lay shivering. His heart was thumping hard. He didn't like the darkness. The house seemed so big when everyone was in bed.

He hugged Lively to him.

"You're better than an old stuffed rabbit," he told her.

But Lively didn't want to be hugged. She had woken up and wanted to explore. She wriggled out of his arms and ran snuffling down by his feet. Mike giggled.

"Stop it, Lively. That tickles."

He kicked with his feet. She ran up his back and came out by his ear. She began to

nibble his hair. Mike pushed her away and she went down the bed again. This was fun! Why don't I have her in bed every night? Mike thought.

They played for some time. Wherever Lively was in his bed, Mike could feel her nose twitching and her soft breath snuffling. Her little claws tickled too. At last, Lively curled up on the pillow and fell asleep. Mike put his arm over her. He snuggled his face close to her furry warmness. It wasn't long before he was asleep too.

When Mike woke up again, he heard Stevie giggling. The sun was shining and the room was bright. Mike stretched. He opened his eyes. Then he sat up in surprise. There on the floor was Stevie – and Lively – and lots of rabbit droppings!

"Oh, no! How did she get in here?" Mike groaned.

Then he remembered. He had gone down and got her in the night.

"Lively, how could you?" he asked.

Then a horrible thought struck him. If she had done that on the floor, what had she done in his bed? He leapt out of bed and flung his duvet back. No droppings, but there was a hole where Lively must have chewed it. He turned back the bottom of his duvet. There on one corner was a little pile of hard brown pellets.

"Yuk!" Mike yelled. "Mum! Mum! Come and see what Lively's done."

Mum came into the room, carrying baby Rachel.

"Mike, what is all this? What is Lively

doing up here? And why is your bed in such a mess?' she asked.

Mike suddenly realised that it was all his fault. He looked at his torn duvet and began to cry.

"I was scared. Stevie had Peter Rabbit and I wanted someone . . ." he said.

Mum held a hand out to Mike.

"Come on, boys. Let's go and have breakfast. We can clear the mess up later. Stevie, can you carry Lively very carefully?

I think she'll be happier back in her hutch," she said.

Mike wiped his eyes on his pyjama sleeve and grabbed Mum's hand. Stevie picked Lively up round her middle. Together they all went downstairs for breakfast.

"I'm sorry," Mike whispered, as Mum gave him a big bowl of cornflakes.

After breakfast, Mum put Rachel down for a sleep. Stevie was watching television.

"Come on, Mike. We've got some tidying up to do," said Mum.

So they went upstairs with all the cleaning things. Mike put the sheet and duvet in the washing machine. Mum cleaned the mess on the floor. When it was all finished, Mum sat on Mike's bed. She patted the place beside her.

"Come and sit down, Mike. Tell me all about it," she said.

Mike tried to explain.

"Stevie had a dream about the big dog. I couldn't stop thinking about it too. I got scared. I needed Peter Rabbit. But Lively helped. I wasn't scared when I had her with me."

"Mike, Lively isn't the same as Peter Rabbit. You can't do the same things with a real rabbit as you can with a toy one. It isn't fair to expect Lively to know how to behave in a bedroom. She doesn't belong there," Mum said gently.

"But I *needed* her," Mike insisted.

"Mike, if you are old enough to have a real rabbit, you are old enough to care for it properly. That means putting her needs before your own. She needs a nice safe hutch where she can behave like a rabbit. When you get scared, you can't expect her to behave like a toy rabbit, can you?" Mum asked.

Mike sighed. "No, I won't do it again," he said.

"Good. Now go and put her in her run in the garden. And see if you can find a nice big dandelion for her,' said Mum.

That night, when Dad was putting him to bed, Mike thought of something.

"Dad, did Mum tell you about this morning?" he asked.

Dad nodded.

"Well, what do I do if I get scared tonight? It isn't fair to have Lively in bed with me."

"No, it isn't. Lively has to be cared for in the way *she* needs. She needs to sleep in a soft wood shaving bed. She should not be squashed under a duvet with you. But God cares for you in just the way *you* need. He sent his son, Jesus, to be with you all the time, even in the middle of the night."

"But I can't cuddle Jesus! He isn't with me like Lively is. I can't see him!"

"No, but you can talk to him. You can ask him to help you not to be afraid. He will do that because he loves you. He will always look after you."

Mike snuggled down in bed. He looked over to where Stevie lay. He was asleep, with Peter Rabbit held tight in his arms.

"I'll pretend Jesus is holding me just like that," he said.

"He is," Dad replied. "The Bible tells us that no one can take us out of Jesus' hands. He holds us even tighter than Stevie holds Peter Rabbit."

Lively Gets Lost

It was fun in the garden. Mum had said that Mike could get Lively out of her run. She could run around the garden while Stevie and Mike were out there to look after her.

Lively was so funny hopping across the lawn. She was very excited to be out. She hopped, she sniffed, she jumped, then . . .

"Oh look, Stevie. She's doing a hop, skip and jump!" Mike said.

"Not a jump! A ping!" Stevie said.

Stevie's way of describing it was best. It was like a "ping"! Lively took two or three little runs and jumps. Then, all at once, she

took a big jump. She turned over in the air as she jumped, with her ears suddenly pointing straight upwards. When she landed, she shook her ears down over her back.

"She really is enjoying the space, isn't she?" Mike said.

"Hop, skip, ping! Hop, skip, ping! Go on, Lively!" he called.

They watched her for a few minutes, then Mike picked her up and took her to one end of the lawn. She ran back across the grass towards Stevie, doing a hop, skip, ping on the way. Then she suddenly turned and went running off into the bushes. Mike and Stevie had to hunt for her. They had a lovely time.

Then Stevie got bored. He went to play in the sandpit. Mike took Lively across. She loved the sand. She dug in it with her little front paws. Then she scraped at it with her back paws. The sand went flying up behind her.

"Look, Stevie. Lively is digging a burrow," Mike said.

"I can dig faster!" yelled Stevie. He picked up a spade and began to dig. The sand went flying up behind him too!

"I can dig faster than both of you," Mike boasted. He grabbed another spade, and sent sand scattering everywhere.

They had a great time in the sand. After they had finished digging, they smoothed the sand into roads. Stevie went indoors to get some cars. Mike stood up. He looked proudly at what they had done. It was the best road layout they had ever made!

Then he remembered. Where was Lively? He had been so busy playing in the sand that he had forgotten all about her. He looked around. He couldn't see her anywhere. He ran over to her run, but she wasn't there. He ran over to the bushes, but she wasn't there. He ran to the back door. She wasn't anywhere there.

Stevie came back out with lots of cars.

"Stevie, I've lost Lively. Please help me look for her," Mike told him, almost crying.

Stevie dropped the cars and ran over to Lively's run.

"She's not here," he said.

"I know she's not. She's lost. She must have run away when we were playing in the sand. We must look for her. You look under the plants and bushes over there. I'll start this side. Then we will meet in the middle. We're bound to have found her by then."

So they started hunting. There were so many places a little brown rabbit could be hiding. Was she in the empty flowerpots? No, there were only spiders and woodlice

there. Was she under the holly bush? Mike didn't think so, but it was so prickly that he didn't push right underneath. Was she behind the garden shed? No, just more spiders and woodlice. She couldn't have got in the compost heap, could she? Mike carefully pulled the cover up to have a look. Out flew lots of tiny flies. There was a yukky smell too, so he shut it again quickly.

Stevie came trotting across the garden with a big ball in his hands.

"Look what Stevie found," he said.

43

"Well done. We lost that ball ages ago. But you are supposed to be looking for Lively," said Mike.

Stevie dropped the ball at Mike's feet and went back. Soon, all Mike could see was his bottom sticking out from among the plants. Mike hoped Mum wasn't watching from the kitchen!

They hunted for a long time but there was no sign of Lively. Mike was getting very worried now. What if she had got out of the garden? What if she had dug a hole somewhere? In next door's garden? What if she had got out to the front? She could get run over. Or that horrid big dog might get her! Mike shivered just to think about it.

Suddenly, he burst into tears. If the big dog got Lively it would all be his fault. He was supposed to take care of her. It was his responsibility, that's what Dad said. It would be his responsibility if the dog ate her. This idea made him cry even more.

Now it was Stevie's turn to get worried.

"Don't cry, Mike," he begged. But Mike couldn't stop.

Stevie ran indoors to get Mum.

"What's the matter, Mike?" she asked.

"Lively's got lost," Mike sobbed.

"Are you sure? She might just be sleeping somewhere."

"We've looked everywhere!"

Mike explained what had happened.

Mum listened carefully, then she went indoors and came out with a carrot and some cabbage leaves.

"We'll put this on the lawn by her run. When Lively gets hungry she will smell them. Then she will come out from wherever she is hiding and eat them," she said.

Mike took some bits to put inside her run too. He left the top open so that she could jump back in.

Mum looked carefully all round the garden.

"I can't see her anywhere. Let's go and have lunch. You can sit by the kitchen window, Mike. Then you will be able to see Lively when she comes out of her hiding place," she said.

So that is what they did. Mike and Stevie had lunch sitting on the window-sill. They dangled their feet into the kitchen sink. They had never been allowed up there before. Normally it would have been fun, but today Mike was too worried to enjoy it.

All through lunch, Mike stared out of the window. Then he went and sat on the back doorstep. Stevie crept up beside him, and pushed Peter Rabbit into his hands. Mike hugged Peter, but it wasn't the same. Peter had stopped being the special friend he used to be. I want a real, live, warm, wriggling rabbit, Mike thought. But Lively did not appear. Mum called Mike to come in and watch the television. But he just stayed sitting on the doorstep, hugging Peter Rabbit.

The long sad afternoon went on and on. At last, Dad came home. He sat on the step beside Mike.

"Why did Lively get lost?" Mike asked, sadly. He didn't think he would ever see her again.

"Well, why do you think?" said Dad slowly.

Mike considered.

"I stopped playing with her. I forgot she was out of her run. She went exploring, and I wasn't there to bring her back. Now she's lost," he said. He began to cry again.

Dad put his arm round Mike.

"You didn't mean to let her get lost," he said. "Most of the time you are very good at looking after Lively. We don't know where she is now, but we do know that Jesus cares. He told a story about a sheep that got lost. The shepherd hunted and hunted till he found it. Let's ask Jesus to keep Lively safe."

So that's what they did.

A little while later, there was a ring on the front doorbell. Stevie ran to answer it.

"Mike!" he yelled, as soon as it was open. "Mike, come quick!"

Mike jumped up from the settee, where he had been sitting miserably, holding Peter Rabbit. Peter fell and went flying into a corner of the floor. Mike rushed into the hall. There was Jonathan, the boy from two doors away. And in his arms was – Lively!

"Lively!" Mike yelled, and grabbed his rabbit. Lively's ears pricked up and her nose began twitching really fast.

Jonathan smiled.

"We thought it must be yours. My mum said you had a rabbit. Small, isn't it?" he said.

"That's because she's a Dwarf rabbit. Thank you for bringing her back. Where did you find her?" Mike said.

"Mum saw it in the garden. She didn't know what it was. She just noticed something run under the bushes. She was worried in case it was a rat. So Dad and I went out to have a look. You know what it was doing? You know those sunflowers we're all growing for the school competition? Well, mine isn't going to win now. Your rotten rabbit has eaten the top right off," Jonathan said.

"Oh, I'm sorry. You can have mine, if you like," Mike said.

"It doesn't matter. Dad said we could plant another seed. It will have time to catch up. But *he's* really cross with your rabbit. It's eaten all his baby lettuce plants. He spent ages putting them out yesterday. Now they're all gone."

Mike felt awful. Jonathan's dad loved his garden. They weren't allowed to play football on Jonathan's lawn in case the ball hit the flowers or vegetables. Of all the places for Lively to run away to!

But then Jonathan giggled. "It was funny watching Dad trying to catch it. We would really be in trouble if we had trodden on the plants as much as Dad did. Every time he thought he had got it, the rabbit just jumped over his hands and escaped again.

It's very fast, isn't it?" Jonathan said.

Mike looked down at Lively. He could feel her heart beating. She's mine, and I've got her back, he thought. "I'll never forget about you again, Lively," he promised.

Then he grinned at Jonathan. "Thanks for bringing her back. Come and see the hutch we made for her," he said.

That night at bedtime, Mike said his prayers. He thanked Jesus for keeping Lively safe, and for bringing her back.

"Mum, it's hard work looking after a real rabbit, isn't it? I have to think about her all the time. I'm not very good at it yet, am I?" he asked.

"You are getting better. Aren't you glad that God knows how to look after us properly? He never lets us get lost," Mum said.

"He knew where Lively was too, didn't he? He's really good at looking after things," Mike said.

"He looks after us because he's our heavenly Father," Mum said.

"I'm glad. I wouldn't like to be lost like Lively was," Mike said sleepily.

Lively Goes to School

"It's the pet show at school tomorrow. I can take Lively, can't I?" Mike asked.

"Of course you can. We can put her in the box from the shop," Mum said.

"But she can't stay in that tiny little box all day. She needs more room than that!" Mike said.

"I can come and get her after I take Stevie to nursery. Will that be long enough?" Mum asked.

"Yes, I think so," Mike said. He was really looking forward to showing Lively to all his friends. I want them to see how tiny she is, he thought. No one believed me when

I said I had a Dwarf rabbit. They all thought I was making it up.

Mike had had Lively for three weeks now. She had grown a little bit, but not much.

The next morning, Mike woke up feeling excited. He got dressed quickly. Then he ran downstairs and went to get Lively.

"Eat your breakfast first!" Mum called after him.

So he turned round and went back to the table. He ate two slices of toast and drank a glass of milk.

"Can I get Lively ready now?" he asked.

Mum smiled.

"Yes, but what are you going to do?" she asked.

"Wait and see!" Mike said.

First Mike had to find the box from the shop. It had special holes in it so that Lively could breathe. He couldn't remember where they had put it when they had brought Lively home. He looked in the garage. It wasn't there. He ran up to his bedroom. It wasn't there. Where could it be? He looked in the toy cupboard. It wasn't there either.

"Mum! Where is Lively's box?" he shouted.

"I don't know. Have you looked in the cupboard under the stairs?" Mum shouted back.

Mike hadn't, so he ran downstairs again. He jumped the bottom three stairs, and landed in a heap!

He jumped up again, and pulled the cupboard door open. Inside, it was a mess.

There was a pile of newspapers. There was a box of empty bottles, waiting to go to the bottle bank. There were lots of welly boots. There were Dad's big black ones. There were Rachel's tiny red ones, and Mike's own blue pair. But he could only see one of Stevie's. Stevie had welly boots like ducks. They had a yellow beak shape at the front. Mike crawled right into the cupboard. He rummaged around till he found the other one. Good, it was there. Then, right at the back, he found a box of toys. He sat amongst all the muddle, in the warm darkness of the cupboard. He began to investigate inside the box. There were lots of small metal cars. They looked very old. The paint was all scratched. He forgot all about Lively and the pet show. He forgot about getting ready for school.

Suddenly Mum shouted, "Mike! Where are you?"

It was so loud he jumped. He poked his head out of the cupboard. Mum was standing at the bottom of the stairs. She was calling up as if he was in his bedroom. No wonder it sounded so loud!

"Here I am!" he said. Now it was Mum's turn to jump.

"What are you doing in there?" she asked.

"Look what I've found," Mike said, showing her one of the old cars.

"Oh, Dad's old cars. I had forgotten they were in there," Mum said.

"Why has Dad got old cars?" Mike asked.

"They were his when he was a little boy. Come on Mike, put them away now.

You can get them out when you come home from school. You can look at them properly then. Did you find the box?" Mum asked.

"Not yet." Mike did not want to admit that he had forgotten all about it.

"Look, here it is." Mum reached over his head and took it off the shelf above him. "It was right at the back. Come on out now and get ready. We must leave in twenty minutes."

Mike took the box and put some wood shavings in it. Then he put a carrot in too, in case Lively got hungry.

He took Lively out of her hutch. Then he took his comb out of his pocket. Gently he combed Lively. It was hard work because her fur was so thick. Mike had never looked at it really closely before. It looked a dark, chocolate colour, but close up, it was speckled different shades of brown.

Underneath, the fur was very soft and downy. It was very hard to comb. Lively pulled away when he tried, so he just slid the comb over the top. When he had finished, her fur was all smooth. Then he put his hand in his pocket again. This time, he pulled out one of Rachel's shiny pink hair ribbons. Carefully he tied it round Lively's neck.

"There, now you're ready! You'll be the best pet there!" he said.

He put her gently into the box.

When they got to school it was even more exciting. Mike's class had been told to go straight into their classroom with their pets. Everyone else had to wait in the playground till the bell went.

The classroom was full of children with pets. Mike's friend, Sarah, had a kitten. Jonathan, from down the road, had two rats in a cage. David even had a goldfish in a bowl. There were lots of gerbils and hamsters. There were three more kittens. Gemma had a dog, but her mum came in with her and held the lead.

The teacher told all the children to sit down. They had to put their boxes and cages on the tables in front of them. It was so exciting! A lot of the pets were making noises. Sarah's kitten was the worst. It made loud yowling howls. Mike did not know that a kitten could make a noise like that! It kept escaping from her arms and she had to run after it. Once it came face to face with Gemma's dog. Then its fur all stuck up on end. It arched its back and spat at

the dog. The dog barked and pulled to chase the kitten. It was quite frightening. Gemma's mum quickly pulled the dog back and their teacher scooped up the kitten.

"Put your hand through his collar and hold him tight, Sarah. Try not to let him go again. Now, who's going to be first to show and tell about their pet?" asked the teacher.

The children came up to the front with their boxes. One at a time, they let the pets out on to the carpet. When it was her turn, Gemma showed how the dog would sit or lie down when she told it to.

Mike enjoyed looking at all the animals. It was fun to see what they all did. It was fun learning how to look after them all.

When it was his turn, he took the box to the front and opened it. He lifted Lively out very carefully. He held her like the man in the pet shop had shown him. He put her down on the carpet in front of him. Lively just sat there, with her nose twitching. She had one ear up and the other down over her back.

"Isn't she small!" some of the children said.

Mike smiled. He felt like saying, "I told you so," but he didn't. He just said, "That's because she's a Dwarf rabbit. She'll never get very big. She's just about the same size as my little brother's toy rabbit."

"Has anyone else got a rabbit?" the teacher asked.

Peter put his hand up.

"I have," he said.

"Bring him up now, and let's compare them. Mike, pick yours up and hold her tight. Peter, don't bring yours too close. We don't want them to fight," the teacher said.

So Peter opened the box. He brought out an *enormous* rabbit with long, floppy ears.

The class gasped.

"Wow, they are different!" someone said.

"I like Mike's best," said Sarah.

So do I, thought Mike, but he didn't say anything.

That night at bedtime, Mike was telling Dad all about the pet show.

"I didn't know that there were so many different kinds of pets. Even the same animals were different," he said.

"What do you mean?" Dad asked.

"Well, Jane's kitten was black and cuddly. But Sarah's kitten was all thin and had a very pointed face. And I thought cats went miaow. Well, Sarah's didn't. It made a very strange yowling noise."

"It sounds like a Siamese," Dad said.

"A sigh-me. That's a strange name, but it was a very strange cat. It was all bony. Peter had a rabbit too. It was about a hundred times bigger than Lively."

"God made lots of different kinds of animals because he wanted a full and interesting world. Imagine if we all had the same pet – if we all had tortoises. That would be boring," Dad said.

"Yes, it was fun seeing all the different ones. Did you know cats don't need to have milk to drink? Water is just as good. They all need different things . . . And the others really liked Lively," Mike added.

"I'm glad you had a good day. God gave you Lively to enjoy. It was nice that your friends could enjoy her too," Dad said.

"I'm going to enjoy a dog, too," Mike said.

Dad groaned, "Not *another* pet!"

"No, Dad. Gemma's mum says I can go to the park with them on Saturday. Gemma's going to show me the dog's tricks," Mike said, laughing.

"That's a relief!" Dad sighed.

Lively Gets Sick

"Why won't she eat anything?" Mike asked. Last night, Lively had not eaten much of her food. This morning, he had given her some more, but she still wouldn't eat it.

"Come on, Lively," Mike begged.

But it was no use. Lively just sat there, not even twitching her nose.

He went to fetch her a carrot. She just looked at it. He ran out into the garden and picked a dandelion leaf. She just looked at that too. Stevie was sitting at the kitchen table with a yoghurt. Mike grabbed the spoon just as Stevie was about to put it in his mouth. Stevie yelled.

"It's for Lively," Mike explained, and ran over to her hutch. Stevie was so surprised that he didn't even complain. But Lively wouldn't eat the yoghurt either. She just sniffed at it, so Mike thrust the spoon back in Stevie's hand. Stevie plunged it into his yoghurt pot and carried on with his breakfast.

Mike went and opened the cupboard. There must be something Lively would like, he thought. There were packets of soup, tins of beans, pasta, Rachel's baby food.

Nothing there for Lively. He opened another door. Packets of crisps, the breakfast cereal, a new packet of biscuits. There was also a packet of chocolate buttons on the shelf. Mike took one button over to Lively. She didn't even sniff at it. Sadly, Mike put the button in his own mouth. Then he picked Lively up. She sat quietly in his arms. He stroked her soft fur. It wasn't as shiny as usual.

"You must eat your food, Lively. You'll get ill if you don't," he whispered.

He put her back in her hutch. She curled up in her sleeping part.

"That's right, have a nice sleep. I'll come and see you as soon as I get home from school," Mike told her.

It was a lovely autumn day. The sun was shining, but it was windy as well. There were little white clouds in the sky. They looked as if they were chasing each other. The wind blew the leaves from the trees. They fell, golden and brown and red, all

around Mike and Mum as they walked to
school. Stevie ran ahead trying to catch
them. He was wearing a thick brown and
red jumper. He looked almost like a big
leaf himself. Rachel laughed as the leaves
danced around her. Sometimes one landed
in the pushchair. Then she laughed even
more.

But Mike didn't feel like laughing. It
should have been a lovely walk to school.
But it wasn't. Mike couldn't stop thinking
about Lively. Why wouldn't she eat? What
was wrong with her? Was she really ill?

Then he remembered something.

"Mum, last winter when Stevie was ill, you took him to the doctor, didn't you?" he asked.

"Yes. Don't you remember? The doctor said he had a sore throat. It hurt so much that Stevie didn't want to eat."

"How did it get better?" Mike wanted to know.

"The doctor gave him some medicine – an antibiotic. I had to give him a spoonful before every meal."

"Oh, yes, I remember. It was pink, and you used that funny plastic spoon," Mike said.

"The spoon came with the medicine. That was to make sure I gave him exactly the right amount," Mum said.

"If Lively isn't better tonight, can we take her to the doctor?" Mike asked. "Maybe she's got a sore throat. She needs some anti bebotic."

Mum laughed.

"Anti-bi-ot-ic," she explained. "But we

would take her to the vet, not the doctor. Doctors are for people. Vets are for animals," she said.

"Well, can we take her anyway?" Mike insisted.

"I'll look after her very carefully today. And if she still isn't better tonight, then we'll take her to the vet," Mum promised.

By now, they had come to the school gate. Rachel waved her hand, as she always did. Stevie ran across the playground towards the nursery. Mike gave Mum a hug, and walked towards his classroom. Some of his

friends were playing football. Mike didn't feel like playing. He was still too worried about Lively.

Then he remembered something. Yesterday at church, the story had been about Jesus. He had learnt that Jesus loves us so we can tell him all our worries.

I bet he loves Lively too, Mike thought. Jesus, please look after Lively.

He felt a bit better then. But all through the day he kept remembering how she wouldn't eat, and how sad she had looked. His teacher kept telling him to stop day-dreaming. Mike tried, but it was hard.

Usually he enjoyed maths and science but today he couldn't concentrate. All he wanted to do was to go home and see how Lively was.

At last, hometime came. Mike ran out of school.

"Mum! How is she? Is she better?" he shouted.

Mum shook her head.

"She has had a little bit to eat, but not much. I think we should take her to the vet," she said.

"Will he made her better?" Mike asked. He couldn't bear the thought of Lively being ill.

"I'm sure he will. I've left Stevie and Rachel at Jonathan's house. His mum is going to give them tea. I've got Lively in the car already. Let's go!" Mum said.

When they got to the vet's, Mike carried Lively's box in. He had never been to the vet's before. In some ways, it was a bit like the doctor's. There was a big desk with a computer on it. A lady in a white coat was standing behind it. There were doors with names on them. There were lots of chairs, with people sitting waiting on them.

But in other ways it was quite different. For a start, everybody had a pet. There were dogs lying on the floor, or sitting on their owners' laps. There were cats, and rabbits, in cages and boxes. And it smelt funny – he had smelt something like that before. It's a bit like the pet shop, Mike remembered.

"It is just like the doctor's. Except for the animals," Mike whispered.

"Well, a vet is an animal doctor," Mum said.

"Can we see him now?" Mike asked.

"Soon. We have to tell the receptionist all about her first," Mum said.

The receptionist behind the desk asked lots of questions about Lively, and about Mike. She typed all the answers on her computer.

At last, she said, "There, that's all we need to know. Go and sit down. The vet will call you when it's your turn."

Mike and Mum went and sat down by the window. Mike put Lively's box on the floor.

He looked around at all the other animals. There was a dog with a big bandage round its leg. There was another dog that looked as if its skin was too big for its body. It had wrinkles everywhere – on its face, down its legs, over its back. The only bit that wasn't wrinkly was its tail! There was a little puppy that kept jumping around and barking. I wonder what's wrong with that one? Mike thought.

"Mum, are all these animals ill?" he asked.

"No, some of them have come to have injections, to stop them getting ill. That puppy is probably only having injections," Mum said.

"Like the one I had for measles last year?" Mike asked.

"That's right. Now you won't get ill with measles," Mum replied.

"Is it to stop that puppy getting measles then?" Mike asked.

"Probably not measles. There are illnesses that dogs can get, and the injection is for them. They all have long names. There's one called distemper," Mum said.

"Can they stop dogs having a bad temper?" Mike asked.

Mum smiled. "I don't think that's what it means," she said.

Just then, the outside door opened and a dog came in wearing a lampshade round its neck!

"Mum! Look, that dog's got a lampshade on!" Mike whispered.

The man with the dog heard him, and smiled.

"It's not a lampshade, it's a special kind of collar. My dog has had an operation. Look, you can see the stitches on his side, here. The collar means he can't get his head round to chew at them. It is giving the wound a chance to heal," the man explained.

Mike looked. On one side of the dog the fur had all been cut away. There were some untidy black stitches in his skin. The dog turned his head to look at Mike. The collar

77

banged his side. It stopped his head going any further. Mike could see how it helped, but the dog looked so sad.

"Doesn't he mind it?" he asked. He didn't get an answer because, just then, a door opened.

A man in a white coat called, "Michael Jones and Lively."

"That's me!"

"Come on then. Bring your mummy with you as well," the vet said.

So they went into the vet's room. Mike put Lively's box on the table. The vet opened the box and took Lively out.

"What is wrong with her?" he asked.

"She won't eat," Mike said.

Mum explained a bit more.

The vet looked at Lively's ears then opened her mouth and looked in it. He listened to her heart with a strange metal thing.

"I think she just has a rabbit cold. We'll give her some antibiotic. Let's see if that will clear it up," he said.

Mike expected him to give them a bottle of medicine. Instead, he gave Lively an injection.

"I thought those were to stop you getting ill. I had one for measles," Mike said.

"Some are. But for small animals, it's a good way to get the antibiotic working quickly. Then it can start making them better straight away," the vet explained.

He smiled at Mike.

"Bring her back at the weekend if you're still worried about her. But I am sure she will be better by then," he said.

And she was! The next day she ate a little bit, and slept a lot. Then the next day she ate a bit more. On Friday morning, she stood up on her back legs to get the food Mike was holding. And her nose was twitching faster than ever.

"I'm so glad you're better. I think Jesus helped the vet to make you well," he said.

Lively's New Clothes

It was raining. It had been raining all week.
Now it was the weekend and it was still
raining. Mike was cross. It should not rain
at the weekend. Dad had promised them a
picnic by the river. It was going to be the
last one before winter came and it got too
cold. Now it was too wet.

Mike was bored as well. He had played
cars with Stevie. He had made a big castle
with his *Lego*. He had played with Rachel.
He had watched lots of things on the telly.
And now he did not know what to do.

Suddenly he thought about Lively. Lively
must be bored too. I'll get her out and play

with her, he decided.

Five minutes later, he was in his bedroom with Lively in his arms. He put her on his bed. As usual, she ran up and down, sniffing and nibbling at his duvet, his pyjamas, his toys. She sniffed at his school library books which were lying on the bed. Mike threw himself down on the bed and opened one.

"Look, Lively, this one is about you," he said. The book told all about how to look after rabbits and the different kinds you could get. There was even a picture of one just like Lively. Mike flipped the pages over

to find it. Lively was more interested in eating the pages than in looking at the picture. So Mike opened the other book. This one was all about dinosaurs. Lively still wasn't interested. Mike wanted to read so he picked Lively up and put her on the floor. She hopped under his bed. Then she started chewing at the corner of his duvet.

"Don't do that," Mike said. "Remember the trouble I got into last time."

He picked Lively up and put her into Stevie's little plastic truck. She looked very funny sitting in the back of it. Mike picked up his baseball cap and put it on her.

"Now she's a real truck driver," he said.

"That's too big!" Stevie objected.

It was! The cap nearly covered Lively. All they could see was the tip of her nose and her little fluffy tail.

"I'll go and get one of Rachel's hats," Mike said.

But when he got to Rachel's room he had an even better idea. There on the shelf was her doll. And the doll had a tiny hat on – just the right size for Lively!

Rachel's doll was very special. Granny had made it for her. It had a little white cap, with lace all round it. It had a long dress with little pink and blue flowers all over it and lace round the bottom. Over the dress there was a white apron. On top of all this there was a red cloak made of soft velvet. It was such a special doll that Rachel didn't play with it yet. It just sat on the shelf and looked beautiful.

Mike reached up and took the doll off the shelf. The hat came off easily. Then he untied the ribbons that held the cloak on. He untied the apron too. The dress had tiny little buttons all down the back. They were very fiddly, but he got them undone at last. He put the doll back on the shelf. Sitting there without her clothes, she didn't look so special any more. Then he picked up the clothes and went back into his own bedroom.

Lively was still sitting in the truck. She seemed to like it there. She was nibbling at Mike's baseball cap.

"Don't do that, Lively!" Mike shouted, grabbing it away from her. There was a little hole in the back.

"Why didn't you stop her, Stevie?" he asked crossly.

"Didn't see!" Stevie mumbled.

Mike picked Lively up. He held the dress up against her. It looked as if it would fit. He put it over her head. Then he pulled her front paws through the arm holes. It was a bit tight round her neck, so he left the top button undone. Lively kept struggling to get away. As Mike did the last button up, she escaped. When she hopped, her little white

tail showed under the lace at the bottom of the dress. She looked so funny that Stevie and Mike started giggling.

Mike picked her up again, and tied the apron on. Lively would not keep still so it was hard to tie the bow. At last it was done, and she hopped away again. But now she kept tripping over the apron. This was even funnier. Mike and Stevie couldn't stop laughing.

Then Lively sat down and began to nibble at the apron. She chewed the bottom at first. Then one of the strings fell forward and she nibbled at that.

"She's trying to take it off," Mike said. That set them off laughing even more.

"I'm going to put the hat on," Mike said. He grabbed Lively and put the hat on her head. It fell off, so he put it on again. It fell off again. This time, he stuffed both her ears into the hat. It stayed on. She looks like the fairy godmother on the *Cinderella* video, Mike thought.

He put Lively into Stevie's truck again.

"She's not a truck driver. Get something else," Stevie said.

"OK," Mike said.

He went back into Rachel's room. What else was there? His eyes fell on the doll, sitting there with only her underclothes on. Suddenly he realised what he had done. Lively was back in his bedroom chewing the doll's clothes!

He rushed back into his own room. Lively was still sitting in the truck, chewing at the hat.

"Oh, no!" Mike groaned, grabbing it

away from her. It was too late. Lively had chewed a hole right in the middle. Mike threw the hat on his bed. I'm in big trouble now, he thought. He picked Lively up and untied the apron. She had chewed that too. There was a hole in the lace. One of the strings was shorter than the other and all frayed at the end. Worse and worse, Mike thought. What is Mum going to say? Mike took the dress off and looked at it. It looked all right. At least she hadn't chewed that, Mike thought.

Mike sat on his bed. What am I going to do? He thought about all the things he could do. I could just dress the doll again and not tell anyone, he thought. But Stevie would know. Stevie might tell. Then I would be in even worse trouble. And even if he didn't tell, Rachel's doll would still be spoilt. I could try to mend the holes. But I'm not very good at sewing. However hard I tried, it wouldn't be as good as Granny's. I could tell Mum. But she would be very cross. But I have to tell her.

The longer Mike sat there, the more he knew that he had to go and tell Mum what he had done. And the more he didn't want to. At last he jumped up. He picked up the clothes and went downstairs.

Mum did not shout at him. She did not seem cross, just sad. She went very quiet. Then she said, "You were very brave to come and tell me. I am proud of you for that. But I *am* very cross that you did such a silly thing. You know how special that doll is. You also know that Lively is not a toy. If you want to dress something up you must use Peter Rabbit. Lively is a real rabbit and rabbits don't like being dressed up in clothes. There are lots of ways you can have fun with her. You must start taking your responsibility seriously. Otherwise, we might think you are not big enough to have a real rabbit of your own. Now I want you to go upstairs and think what you can do to put it all right."

Mike went sadly out of the room. If Mum had shouted at him it might not have been so bad. Now he just felt that he had let her down. I don't want them to take Lively away, he thought.

He sat down on the stairs. How could he make it all right? He couldn't! The clothes were spoilt. But Granny could mend them. Mike sat a bit longer. Then he stood up and went back to Mum.

"Can I phone Granny? I'll tell her how the clothes got spoilt, and ask her if she can mend them. And I'm sorry, Mum. Please don't take Lively away from me. I will try to look after her properly. I am big enough, really I am," Mike said.

Mum smiled and opened her arms. Mike

ran into them. She gave him a big hug. Mike knew that he was forgiven.

That night at bedtime, Dad talked to Mike about saying sorry.

"When we say sorry to Jesus for the things we have done wrong, he forgives us. Then if we ask him, he will help us not to do wrong things again," he said.

"I said sorry to Mum and Rachel, but I didn't say sorry to Jesus," Mike said.

"Well, I think Jesus knows you are sorry. But when you say your prayers tell him anyway," Dad said.

After Dad went downstairs, Mike lay there for a little while, thinking. Across the room, Stevie lay in his bed. He was asleep, with Peter Rabbit cuddled tight. The door was open and Mike could just see into Rachel's room. She was fast asleep too.

Mike slipped quietly out of bed and tiptoed downstairs to Lively's hutch. She was asleep too. Mike stroked her gently.

"I'm sorry, Lively. I won't dress you up

again," he whispered.

Then he thought about what Dad had said.

"Lord Jesus, please help me to look after Lively just like you look after me. Help me to take proper care of my real rabbit," he whispered.

Other titles in the Read by Myself series

Nobody's Dog

Eleanor Watkins

"There's that dog again," said Luke. Lots of dogs were being walked, because it was Sunday afternoon. Some were on leads and some were off, chasing balls or sticks or just running. But this dog was all on its own.

Luke cannot forget the lonely dog with its hungry brown eyes. It seems to be nobody's dog, so Luke and his friend Mr Bronzovi decide to look after it. But it is not as easy as Luke thinks.

Kangaroo Daniel and the Canal Holiday

Dilys Gower

Ashley wasn't sure he'd heard properly. Take Daniel on holiday with them! Kangaroo Daniel in *his* cabin, sleeping in one of *his* bunk beds, bouncing all over everywhere.

He opened his mouth to say "No!" as loudly as he could but Mum was not waiting to hear what he thought.

Kangaroo Daniel usually causes disasters wherever he goes but on the canal holiday he ends up rescuing Ashley.

Amy T and Grandma B

Eileen Taylor

Amy T hung on to Matthew's jumper as he rushed across the huge showroom.

"Here it is," he said.

Amy T walked round a very large box which was open at the top. Inside were hundreds of light, hollow balls. "Come on! Climb in!" said Matthew, who was already diving amongst the balls.

All sorts of fun things happen when Amy T and Matthew visit Grandma B.

The Other Kitten

Patricia St John

Mark and Carol are enjoying a spring holiday at Gran's house by the seaside. One day they see a notice on a gate, offering free kittens and go to investigate.

Mark picked up a black kitten with four white paws and a white nose. "We'll have this one," he said.

"No," said Carol, picking up a grey tabby, "we're having this one, and I'll call it Fluff because it's so soft." Mark and Carol's quarrel over choosing a kitten nearly ends in disaster.

Friska my Friend

Patricia St John

When Colin discovers the hungry dog left at the empty cottage he persuades his parents to let him keep her while her owner is in hospital.

Colin ran to the house. The dog came barking to greet him – he flung his arms round her neck. "You're mine and I'm going to call you Friska," he whispered.

Colin's special friendship with Friska helps him to understand what "you are mine" really means.